Oxford Ink

an innovative approach to English language learning

Book 4

Part B

Gayatri Khanna

OXFORD
UNIVERSITY PRESS

OXFORD
UNIVERSITY PRESS

Oxford University Press is a department of the University of Oxford.
It furthers the University's objective of excellence in research, scholarship, and education by publishing worldwide. Oxford is a registered trade mark of Oxford University Press in the UK and in certain other countries.

Published in India by
Oxford University Press
YMCA Library Building, Jai Singh Road, New Delhi 110001, India

First published in 2017
Second impression 2017

ISBN-13: 978-0-19-947032-7
ISBN-10: 0-19-947032-4

Typeset in Univers LT Std 55 Roman
by Aptara Techbooks International Pvt. Ltd, Noida 201301
Printed in India by Manipal Technologies Ltd., Karnataka 576104

Illustrations by Aptara Techbooks International Pvt. Ltd

Introduction

Oxford Ink: an innovative approach to English language learning **is a new communicative course with a fresh and contemporary approach to learning. Embedded in the course are universal values of social justice and truth with focus on the inherent diversity of India as well as global themes relevant to our students. The course is designed to reduce the curriculum load while providing a high quality, stimulating learning experience, that is joyful, creative and participative.**

SPECIAL FEATURES OF *OXFORD INK*

1

Carefully designed course curriculum

- lighter curriculum with greater focus on higher order thinking skills
- perfect balance of reading texts, exercises, CCE material and integrated practice worksheets

2

Wide-ranging reading texts from India and around the world

- classic and contemporary prose and poetry selections
- students are exposed to reading formats that they will encounter in real life: magazine articles, book and film reviews, advertisements, blogs, interviews, diary entries, cartoons, news reports

3

Interlinked skill-based exercises

interlinking LSRW skill-based exercises across the unit to help learners apply skills cross-functionally

4

Assessments for feedback and remedial action

Ongoing and differentiated evaluation through:

- Formative assessment
- Summative assessment
- Problem solving assessment
- Assessment of speaking and listening
- OTBA
- Projects
- Life skills
- Self and peer assessment
- Value-based in-text and comprehension questions

5

Comprehensive grammar syllabus

carefully graded grammar syllabus includes extensive explanations, practice and extension exercises that make ***Oxford Ink*** a self-sufficient language learning course

6

Building communication skills

integrated listening and speaking activities to build and improve all-round communication skills

7

Value-based learning

integration of value-based learning, with a variety of tools to reinforce constitutional, scientific, personal, interpersonal, global and eternal values across the series

COURSE COMPONENTS

A **Warm-up** activity in each unit or prose lesson introduces the students to the essence of the units.

Reading selections comprise classic texts of high literary merit from across India and the world in a variety of formats.

Comprehension questions, in each prose lesson, ranging from factual and inferential to extrapolative and value-based, aid in global and selective understanding of the texts.

Word power sections, derived from the reading lessons, help in acquisition, retention and retrieval of new and known words through a wide assortment of tasks.

Grammar check sections, also derived from the reading lessons, combine the best of descriptive and prescriptive methods. Analysis of usage and detailed explanation, combined with exhaustive exercises in the units and the worksheets offer a comprehensive grammar programme for the students.

Study skills sections include lessons in pronunciation, punctuation, dictionary work, spelling and idioms to ensure all-round proficiency.

Write now sections prompt students to practice both formal and informal writing with particular emphasis on form.

Communication corner sections combine the honing of listening and speaking skills in one module—listening tasks based on authentic language experiences cover a wide range of listening skills, and speaking tasks are extensions of the listening tasks.

Worksheets follow every unit to provide additional practice for the grammar and writing topics covered in the unit.

Poems have been carefully selected to make poetry lessons more enjoyable than intimidating while the **appreciation** sections cover the formal aspects of teaching and learning of poetry.

Literature Readers are designed to get students to read and enjoy quality texts. They contain a wide range of prose and poetry selections from around the world.

TEACHER'S RESOURCE PACK

Teacher's Resource Pack comprises Teacher's Resource Book, Audio CD and Oxford Educate with Test Generator.

Teacher's Resource Book provides teachers with pedagogical notes, handy lesson plans, listening scripts and answer keys.

Audio CD has audio for listening exercises and poems.

DIGITAL SUPPORT

Oxford educate For Teachers

Features of Oxford Educate:

- **Animations** of poems
- **Interactive exercises** based on content from the text
- **Audio** for prose, poems, glossary, listening exercises and pronunciation
- **Lesson plans** for each unit (printable)
- **Answer keys** for each unit (printable)
- **Worksheets** which can be used as practice or classroom assignments (printable)
- **Slide shows** for dynamic explanation of key topics
- **Reference sheets** containing images and additional information
- **Video clips** for visual learning

Oxford Educate is an innovative digital resource that provides teachers with an e-book integrated with learning materials and interactive tools. The package also includes an easy-to-use Test Generator for effective evaluation.

Oxford Areal

Oxford **Areal** is a magical app that makes your textbook come alive! The digital content can be accessed through the ▶ icon marked on the relevant pages.

Setting up and using the free Oxford Areal app is easy. Simply follow the steps given below.

1. Search and install the free Oxford Areal app from the App Store (iOS)/Play Store (Android).
2. Run the app and locate your book using the SEARCH box.

3. Tap the book cover to select it.

4. Tap GET THIS BOOK.
5. Tap SCAN and scan any page that has the ▶ icon. Tap DOWNLOAD to save the Oxford Areal content for that page.
6. Once you have scanned and downloaded a page, you will be able to view the digital content linked to it offline. To do so, simply tap the cover of the book and then the scanned page. To scan a new page, tap SCAN.

Oxford AREAL contains

- **Animations** of poems
- **Games** based on grammar and vocabulary topics
- **Short video clips** for reference
- **Interactive exercises** based on glossary

Contents

Detailed Contents

Chapter	Vocabulary	Grammar	Study skills	Writing	Listening	Speaking
5. Fair Play Worksheet 5	Synonyms and antonyms	Tenses: Simple Past, Past Continuous, Simple Future and Future Continuous ✓	Dictionary skills: Using a thesaurus	Writing a diary entry ✓	Listening to a story on Shibi Rana	Speaking to resolve conflicts
6. Anansi and Turtle Share Dinner Worksheet 6	Words related to a restaurant	Subject verb agreement ✓	Language skills: Fact vs. Opinion	Writing an invitation ✓	Listening to a conversation on eating at a restaurant	Problem solving through role-play
My Computer Ate My Homework						
7. Gulliver in the Land Of Giants Worksheet 7	Synonyms from the text	Modals: *Can* and *May* ✓	Language skills: Compound words	Writing an informal letter ✓	Listening to the description of a fantasy creature	Role-play on kindness
8. Too Many Professors Worksheet 8	Synonyms	Adverbs of degree ✓	Pronunciation: /s/ and /sh/ sounds	Describing an imaginary invention ✓	Listening to a poem	Conversation through role-play
The Little Big Man						
9. How The First Letter was Written Worksheet 9	Animal idioms	Conjunctions ✓	Punctuation: Comma	Making a poster ✓	Listening to a passage on the Stone Age	Discussing the basic tools of the Stone Age
Dear Mum						

Formative Assessment 2

Formative Assessment 3

Life Skills 2

Assessment of Speaking and Listening

Summative Assessment 2

Open Text-Based Assessment

Acknowledgements

'Mr. Brown the Circus Clown' copyright © 2012 Kenn Nesbitt. All Rights Reserved. From *The Armpit of Doom*. Purple Room Publishing. Reprinted by permission of the author; 'Fair Play' by Munshi Premchand translated by Ruth Vanita from *The Co-Wife and Other Stories* published by Penguin Books; 'Dear Mum' from *Thawing Frozen Frogs* by Brian Patten. Published by Penguin, 1989. © Brian Patten. Reproduced by permission of the author c/o Rogers, Coleridge and White Ltd., 20 Powis Mewis, London W11 1JN; 'My Computer Ate My Homework' © 2005 by Kenn Nesbitt. Reprinted from *When Teacher Isn't Looking* with the permission of Meadowbrook Press

The publishers have applied for permission to the following:

Every effort has been made to contact the owners of the copyright of the pieces published here. However, a few have been difficult to trace. It would be appreciated if the copyright owners of the following pieces could contact the publishers:

Florence Tuttle for 'My Books and I'; Norman Hunter for 'Too Many Professors'

Appropriate acknowledgements will be made in future editions of the book.

Photographs

Andy Green/Getty Images (Cave painting pg.155); Walter Myers/Stocktrek Images/Getty Images (New Horizons spacecraft pg.15); moodboard/Getty Images (Female eskimo pg. 16); Smit/Shutterstock (Igloo pg.17)

5. Fair Play

Warm-up

1. **What does being fair mean to you?**
   - Playing by the rules
   - ……………………………………………………………
   - ……………………………………………………………

2. **Have you ever been treated unfairly? If yes, how did you feel? Narrate the incident.**

Now read this story on being fair.

Jumman Sheikh and Algu Chowdhary were good friends. So strong was their bond of friendship that when either of them went away from the village, the other looked after his family. Both were greatly respected in the village.

Jumman had an old aunt who had some property. This she transferred to Jumman on the understanding that she would stay with him and he would look after her. The agreement worked well for a couple of years. Then the situation changed. Jumman and his family were tired of the old relative. Jumman became indifferent to her while his wife grudged[1] even the little food that the old lady wanted every day. The old lady swallowed these insults along with her food for a few months. But patience has its limits.

One day she spoke to Jumman. 'My son, it is now clear that I am not wanted in your house. Kindly give me a monthly allowance so that I can set up a separate kitchen.'

[1]**grudged:** thought that somebody does not deserve to have something expected

'My wife knows best how to run the house. Be patient,' said Jumman shamelessly.

This made his aunt very angry and she decided to take her case to the village *panchayat*[2].

For many days, the old lady was seen talking to the villagers, explaining her case and seeking their support. At last, she came to Algu Chowdhary and spoke to him. 'You know, *Chachi*, Jumman is my best friend. How can I go against him?' said Algu. 'But is it right, my son, to keep quiet and not say what you consider just and fair?' pleaded the old lady. 'Come to the *panchayat* and speak the truth,' she said. Algu didn't reply, but her words kept ringing in his ears.

The *panchayat* was held the same evening under an old banyan tree. Jumman stood up and said, 'The voice of the *panch*[3] is the voice of God. Let my aunt nominate the head-*panch*. I will accept her decision.'

'The *panch* knows neither friend nor enemy. What do you say to Algu Chowdhary?' the old lady announced.

[2]**panchayat**: a village council | [3]**panch**: member of the *panchayat*

'Fine,' replied Jumman, hiding his joy over this unexpected piece of luck.

'*Chachi*, you are aware of my friendship with Jumman,' said Algu.

'I know that,' replied the aunt, 'but I also know that God lives in the heart of the *panch* and his voice is the voice of God.' And the old lady explained her case.

'Jumman,' said Algu, 'you and I are old friends. Now I am a *panch*. You and your aunt are equal before me. What do you have to say in your defence?'

'Three years ago,' began Jumman, 'my aunt transferred her property to me. I promised to support her as long as she lived. I have done all I could. There have been a couple of quarrels between my wife and her but I can't stop it. Now my aunt is claiming a monthly allowance from me. This is not possible. That's all I have to say.'

Jumman was questioned in the *panchayat* by Algu and others. Then Algu announced, 'We have gone into the matter carefully. In our opinion, Jumman must pay his aunt a monthly allowance, or else the property goes back to her.'

Now, the two friends were seldom seen together. The bond of friendship between them was broken. In fact, Jumman was Algu's enemy and wanted his revenge.

Days passed and as ill luck would have it, Algu Chowdhary found himself in a difficult position. One of his fine pair of bullocks[4] died, and he sold the other to Samjhu Sahu, a cart driver of the village. The understanding was that Sahu would pay the price of the bullock in a month's time. It so happened that the bullock died within a month.

Several months after the bullock's death, Algu reminded Sahu of the money he hadn't yet paid. Sahu got very annoyed. 'I can't pay you a penny for the sickly beast you sold me. He brought us nothing but bad luck. I have a bullock. Use it for a month and then return it to me. No money for the dead bullock,' he said angrily.

Algu decided to refer the case to the *panchayat*. The *panchayat* was held under the old banyan tree. Algu stood up and said, 'The voice of the *panch* is the voice of God. Let Sahu nominate the head-*panch*. I will abide by[5] his decision.'

Sahu saw his chance and proposed the name of Jumman. Algu's heart sank and he turned pale. But what could he do?

The moment Jumman became head-*panch*, he realized his responsibility as judge and the dignity[6] of his office. He thought and thought. He must not allow his personal feelings to come in the way of speaking the truth and doing justice.

Both Algu and Sahu stated their cases. They were interrogated[7] and the case was considered deeply. Then Jumman stood up and announced, 'It is our opinion that Sahu should pay Algu

[4]**bullock:** a young bull | [5]**abide by:** to accept and act according to a law or an agreement | [6]**dignity:** honour and respect given by people | [7]**interrogated:** asked many questions over a long period of time

the price of the bullock. When Sahu bought the bullock, it suffered from no disability or disease. The death of the bullock was unfortunate but Algu cannot be blamed for it.' Algu could not contain his feelings. He stood up and said loudly over and over again. 'Victory to the *panchayat*. This is justice. God lives in the voice of the *panch*.'

Soon after, Jumman came to Algu, embraced him and said 'Since the last *panchayat*, I had become your enemy. Today I realised what it meant to be a *panch*. A *panch* has neither friend nor enemy. He knows only justice. Let no one deviate[8] from the path of justice and truth for friendship or enmity[9].

Algu embraced[10] his friend and wept. And his tears washed away all the dirt of misunderstanding between them.

Premchand (retold)

[8]**deviate:** to do something in a different way from what is usual or expected | [9]**enmity:** feelings of hatred | [10]**embraced:** hugged

Munshi Premchand (1880–1936) was a writer of modern Hindi and Urdu literature. He has written about 300 short stories, several novels, many essays and letters. He has also written some plays. Many of Premchand's stories have been translated into English and Russian.

Read and answer

1. Jumman Sheikh and Algu Chowdhary were good friends. Give evidence from the story.
2. How had Jumman Sheikh been unfair to his aunt?
3. Why did the old lady approach Algu Chowdhary? What response did she get?
4. Why was Jumman Sheikh happy with his aunt's decision to nominate Algu Chowdhary as the head-*panch*?
5. How did Jumman Sheikh respond to Algu Chowdhary's judgement?
6. Why did Samjhu Sahu nominate Jumman as the head-*panch*?
7. What was the decision of Jumman? How did Algu react to it?

8. There are two problems in the story, involving two characters each. Fill in this graphic organizer to detail the problems and solutions.

Characters and Cause

1. ....

....

....

2. ....

....

....

....

Problem

....

....

....

....

Solution

....

....

....

Characters and Cause

1. ....

....

....

2. ....

....

....

....

Problem

....

....

....

....

Solution

....

....

....

Think and answer

1. Why do you think the Aunt nominated Algu Chowdhary as the head-*panch*?
2. 'Victory to the *panchayat*. This is justice. God lives in the voice of the *panch*.' Justify this statement with evidence from the story. VB
3. *Algu embraced his friend and wept.* Write a conversation between the two friends explaining what happened after this.

Word power

Match these words from the story with their synonyms and antonyms. You may use the dictionary.

Word	Synonym	Antonym
bond	resented	clash
indifferent	questioned	reply
grudged	sometimes	adhere
seldom	digress	accepted
interrogated	link	concerned
deviate	uncaring	always

Grammar check

Simple past and past continuous tense

Read the following.

Algu's heart sank and he turned pale.

Verbs that speak of actions that took place sometime in the past are said to be in the **simple past tense**.

The **simple past tense** is used:

1. to show actions that took place in the past but are now over
2. to talk about habits that people had in the past

Forming **simple past tense**:

- Sometimes we add **ed** to the main (root) verb.
- If the verb ends in **e**, we just add **d**.
- Sometimes the simple past tense form of the verb is very different from the root verb.
- For some verbs, the simple present and past forms are the same.

We use the **past continuous tense** to:

1. tell us about something that was happening or going on for a short period of time.
2. express an action which was interrupted by another action in the past tense.
3. to describe the scene at the time when the action began.

We form the past continuous tense in the following ways.

- With plural nouns or we/you/they+were+verb+*ing*
- With singular nouns or I/he/she/it+was+verb+*ing*

A. Tick the correct choice of the word to use past continuous tense or simple past tense appropriately.

1. We (are/was/were) sleeping when the bell rang.
2. I (am/was/were) playing with my dog.
3. Yesterday, I (is/was/were) travelling to Mumbai.
4. Rinky (is/was/were) washing the dishes.
5. The children (are/were/was) enjoying the show.
6. The driver (is/was/were) blowing the horn.

B. Frame sentences using the past continuous tense.

1. my dog/bark/at stranger
2. I/knit/pullover
3. we/prepare/examination
4. Anita/travel/Kerala
5. students/dancing/stage
6. Principal/motivate/students

Simple future tense

Simple future tense is used to express an action that has not yet occurred and will occur in the future.

To form a simple future tense, we use 'will' or 'shall' with the main verb in a sentence.

Future continuous tense is used to express an action that is taking place or is being done at that moment, but the action will not have finished at the moment. We use 'will be' with the main verb + *ing* to form the future continuous tense.

C. Fill in the blanks with simple future tense of the verbs given in brackets.

1. I .... at the party tonight. (sing)
2. Sharad .... the university next year. (join)
3. I .... my assignment in an hour. (finish)
4. We .... our dinner at 6 p.m. (eat)
5. The team .... the match next week. (play)
6. The workers .... the structure this week. (build)
7. I .... in class 5 next year. (be)
8. The seed .... into a tree one day. (grow)

Dictionary skills

Using a thesaurus

Find another word for the word in the bracket to complete each of the following phrases. The synonym must begin with the letters given in bold. You could use a thesaurus. One has been done for you.

1. a ....frightened.......... man (terrified)
2. an **im** .... ruler (fair)
3. a **br** .... student (bright)
4. a **fr** .... rose (sweet-smelling)
5. a **de** .... meal (tasty)
6. a **mis** .... child (naughty)

Write now

Diary entry

Are you fair to others? Can you recall an incident when you were fair/unfair to someone? How did you feel after that? Narrate the incident as a dairy entry.

Remember: A diary entry expresses personal feelings

Format for diary entry:

Date: *7th June 2010* or *7 June, or Monday, 7June*

Opening: *Dear Diary,*

Introduction: Could be a general comment on how the day was.

Today was a great day! or *Today was an uninteresting day.*

Body: This is the main part of the diary entry. You could describe what happened to you or express your personal feelings about something or someone.

Conclusion: The diary entry can be concluded with a comment about the day or the situation at that moment or about the lessons learnt.

It was overall an exciting day.

Communication corner

A. Listen to the passage and tick the correct answer.

1. Shibi Rana was known for his
   a. honesty. ☐ b. valour. ☐ c. wealth. ☐
2. The dove was being chased by
   a. a soldier. ☐ b. a king. ☐ c. an eagle. ☐
3. The eagle asked the king to
   a. give the dove. ☐ b. give it food. ☐ c. not be cruel. ☐
4. The king offered the eagle
   a. the dove. ☐ b. the throne. ☐ c. himself. ☐
5. The dove became heavier because
   a. it was evil. ☐ b. it was testing the king. ☐ c. it wanted teach the king a lesson. ☐

B. In the story you just heard, you learnt about selflessness and kindness. Now look at the following pictures. What will you say to these children? How will you resolve these conflicts? Tell the class.

Worksheet 5

Grammar check

Simple past tense and past continuous tense

To form the simple past tense:

- Sometimes, we add ***ed*** to the main (root) verb.
  walk – walked, talk - talked
- If the verb ends in ***e***, we just add ***d***.
  close – closed, taste - tasted
- Sometimes the simple past tense form of the verb is very different from the root verb.
  eat – ate, run – ran, draw – drew, sing – sang, go – went, bring – brought, give – gave, catch – caught, think – thought, win – won, fly – flew, draw – drew
- For some verbs, the simple present and past forms are the same.
  I *read* the newspaper daily. (present)

  I *read* the newspaper in the morning. (past)

  The verb **read** has the same spelling in both sentences but is pronounced differently. In the present tense, **read** is pronounced as reed (to rhyme with **feed**). In the past tense, **read** is pronounced as **red**.
- If a verb ends with y, we replace the **y** with **ied**.
  try – tried, cry – cried
- Sometimes, if a verb ends with **l**, **b**, or **t** we repeat the last letter and add **ed**.
  pat – patted, travel – travelled

A. Use the pictures and words to form interesting sentences in past tense. One has been done for you.

1. My grandmother thought of me when she read my letter.
2. ....
3. ....
4. ....
5. ....
6. ....
7. ....
8. ....
9. ....

We use the past continuous tense to:

1. show an action that was going on (or continuing) in the past.
    - The sun **was shining** bright.
2. show an action that was going on when something else happened.
    - I **was working** when the bell rang.

We form the past continuous tense by

- **was/were** + verb + ing

The **past continuous tense** is used to express an action that was happening at a particular time in the past.

B. Fill in the blanks with verbs in simple past or past continuous. One has been done for you.

1. What .... you .... (doing) last evening?
   Ans: What ....were......... you ....doing......... last evening?
2. He .... (talk) on the telephone when the bell rang.
3. My father .... (meet) people when the call came.
4. The chef .... (cook) a delicious meal for us, yesterday.
5. The police .... (chase) the thief but he .... (jump) over the wall and .... (escape).
6. I .... (walk) towards the library when a dog .... (bite) me.
7. The dogs .... (bark) at me as they had not .... (see) me before.
8. The gardener .... (plant) flowers when it started raining.

9. I .... (try) hard but could not succeed.
10. My friend and I .... (practice) for the maths test, last week.
11. She .... (sleep) when the thieves broke into the house.
12. I ....(listen) to some music, as I .... (wash) the dishes.
13. The actor .... (wave) to the crowd.

Write now

We see and read about people performing heroic deeds every day. In fact all of us are heroes as we do good deeds without even realizing that it is an act of courage. For example: helping a person/an animal in need, saving someone, giving up something to make someone happy.

Recall a heroic deed that you have done. What did you do? How did you feel after that? What did others feel? Write it in the form of a dairy entry. Describe it by selecting just the right adjectives that will help paint a complete and accurate picture. This will help the reader visualize the physical details, but also other important personal attributes. You may use words such as: admire; esteem; respect; look up to; treasure; follow; value; cherish; appreciate; model; measure; venerate; embrace etc.

Day **Date** **Time**

Dear Diary,

This has been one of the most memorable days of my life.

6. Anansi and Turtle Share Dinner

Warm-up

1. **Mention three ways to show respect to yourself.**
   - ....
   - ....
   - ....

2. **Frame three classroom rules to show respect to others.**
   - ....
   - ....
   - ....

Now read about Anansi, the greedy trickster.

One day Anansi[1], the spider, picked some tasty yams[2] from his garden and baked them with much care. 'Umm, they smell delicious!' said Anansi, as he laid a pewter[3] plate, knife and fork on his table.

Just then there was a knock at his door. Anansi peeked out of the window and saw Turtle. Anansi frowned.

Turtle had been travelling all day. His feet were sore, his throat was parched[4], his eyes were dusty and his stomach was empty. However, his nose had told him that Anansi was home and cooking yams for dinner. So Turtle proceeded up the walk to his friend's house.

[1]**Anansi:** pronounced Ah-naan-see | [2]**yams:** the large root of a tropical plant that is cooked as a vegetable | [3]**pewter:** a grey metal made by mixing tin with lead | [4]**parched:** very dry

'Hello, Anansi,' said Turtle politely. 'I have been walking for so long and I smelled the delicious yams. Would you be so kind as to share your meal with me, my dear friend?'

Anansi felt defeated. There was nothing he could do, but welcome Turtle to his house, as it was the custom in his country to share your meal with visitors at mealtime. But Anansi was not happy, for he was a little too greedy and wanted the meal all to himself.

'Please come in, Turtle. I would be honoured to have you as my guest this evening. Sit down and help yourself.'

But just as Turtle crawled up to the table and placed a napkin on his lap. Anansi had a brainwave[5] and bellowed[6] out. 'Wait! In my culture, a guest is expected to come to the table with clean hands. Go down to the creek[7] and wash up.'

[5]**brainwave**: a sudden good idea | [6]**bellowed:** shouted in a loud deep voice, especially because you are angry | [7]**creek:** a small river or stream

Well, of course Turtle's hands were dirty—he'd been crawling on them all day. So he trekked down to the creek behind Anansi's house to wash.

Turtle cleaned his feet as well. He walked all the way back up to the house and Anansi had already begun to eat.

'I didn't want these tasty yams to get cold, so I had to begin,' said Anansi. 'But please do join me now, Turtle.'

Turtle sat down again and reached for a yam, but again Anansi yelled at him.

'Turtle, did you not hear me before? How can you be so rude!' scolded Anansi. 'Didn't I tell you it's not polite to come to my table with dirty hands? Didn't I ask you to wash them? Please do that!'

He looked down and saw that his clean hands had turned dirty once more, since he had to crawl on them to get back to the house. So he walked down to the river once more to wash himself off. And when he returned this time, he was careful to walk on the grass so his hands would stay clean. But by the time he sat down at the table, Anansi had finished up the last bit of the tasty yams and not so much as a morsel[8] was left.

Turtle looked at Anansi for a moment and then said, 'Thank you for sharing your meal with me. If you ever find yourself near my house, please let me return the favour.' And then he slowly walked out the door and continued on his way.

[8]**morsel:** a small amount or a piece of something, especially food

The days went by and Anansi thought more and more of that meal that Turtle had offered. He was interested in a free dinner and finally set off one day to find Turtle's house.

He found Turtle sunning himself on a riverbank just around dinner time.

Turtle looked up and saw him and said, 'Hello, Anansi, have you come to share an evening meal with me?'

'Oh yes, yes!' said Anansi greedily.

As Turtle went to his underwater house to set up the dinner table for the two of them, Anansi stood waiting. He was growing hungrier and hungrier by the minute. Soon Turtle came back to the bank and said, 'The food is ready. Please join me, Anansi.'

And then he dived underwater and began to slowly eat his meal.

Anansi jumped into the water, but could not get down to the bottom of the river. He tried to swim down, but he was so light that he kept popping back up to the surface like a cork. He tried diving. He tried bellyflops[9]. He tried a running jump, but nothing would help him get down to the river bottom.

In the meantime, Turtle was slowly eating his meal.

[9]**bellyflops:** a bad dive into water, in which the front of the body hits the water flat

Anansi was not about to give up a free meal and was running around wondering what he could do. Finally he had an idea. He started grabbing stones and rocks and stuffed them into his jacket pockets.

Now when he jumped into the water he sank right down to the bottom and was able to take his place at the table.

The table was so beautiful and full of delicious foods. Anansi could hardly believe how many tasty foods were before him and could not wait to start his meal.

But just as he reached for the first morsel, Turtle spoke. 'In my country, we do not wear our jackets to the table.'

Anansi noticed that Turtle had removed his own jacket before sitting down. But as soon as Anansi's jacket was off of his shoulders, he went zooming back up to the surface and popped out onto the riverbank.
He stuck his head down into the water and saw Turtle slowly enjoying that wonderful banquet[10].

[10]**banquet**: a large impressive meal

An African folktale

Read and answer

1. Fill in the events of the story.

First

Turtle visits Anansi. Anansi plots...

Turtle has to return hungry, but...

Anansi decides...

Anansi gets an idea...

Turtle tells Anansi to...

Finally

2. *'Would you be so kind as to share your meal with me, my dear friend?'*
   a. Who said this line? Who is the friend?
   b. Where is the speaker coming from?
   c. What happens immediately after this?
3. *He tried bellyflops. He tried a running jump, but nothing would help him get down to the river bottom.*
   a. Who is 'he'? Where is 'he'?
   b. Why is 'he' there?
   c. Why is 'he' engaging in such strange behaviour?

Think and answer

1. Who do you think was smarter of the two? Why?
2. Turtle thanks Anansi and invites him to dinner. Why do you think Turtle is so polite?
3. Imagine Anansi and Turtle meet each other, a few days later. What do you think will they say to each other? Plan a conversation of 8-10 sentences. VB
4. *What goes around, comes around.* This proverb means you have to face the consequences of your actions. Justify the proverb, with examples from the story. VB

Word power

Complete this conversation about ordering in a restaurant. Use the words given below.

menu speciality dessert chef meal order special bill

Waiter: Good evening, are you ready to .... or do you need a little more time?

Customer: Yes. May I have the .... card, please?

Waiter: Sure, here it is.

Customer: What is your .... ?

Waiter: It's continental food, sir.

Customer: Have you any .... meals today?

Waiter: Yes, sir. It's the vegetarian platter.

Customer: That will be good.

In a while.

Waiter: Did you enjoy your .... , sir?

Customer: Yes. You must thank the .... It was a delicious meal.

Waiter: Thank you, sir. Would you like some .... ?

Customer: No, thank you. Can I have .... the please?

Waiter: Sure, sir. In a moment.

Grammar check

Subject-verb agreement

Look at these sentences:

Anansi eats all the food himself.
Anansi and Turtle sit together at the table.

She plays the violin at night.
They walk to the school every day.

Subject-verb agreement means that the subject and verb in a sentence must agree in number.

In most cases the plural form of a noun has an *s* at the end. Boy—Boys

Verbs don't follow this pattern, though. Since *she* is a singular pronoun, *plays* is a singular verb. The word *they* is plural so *walk* is the plural form.

For a verb we add an *s* to make it singular.

1. A verb agrees with its subject in number. Singular subjects take singular verbs. Example: The **toys were** broken.
2. The number of the subject (singular or plural) is not changed by words that come between the subject and the verb. Example: **One** of the toys **is** broken.

1. Match the two halves to form correct sentences.

Column A	Column B
a. The aliens	were in the meadow.
b. The captain and his team	cure patients.
c. The cattle	work hard in building a road.
d. The flowers	carves out beautifully.
e. The lights	travel on a spaceship.
f. The doctors	make noise.
g. The people	acts well.
h. Antonio, the sculptor	are put up to beautify the hall.
i. The girls in the dance class	teach at a school.
j. The actor	were on the playfield.
k. My sisters	is playing cricket.
l. My brother	were switched off at 10 p.m.

2. **Write the subjects and verbs from the sentences in the space below. Also write if they are singular or plural. One has been done for you.**

Subject	Verb	Singular/plural
a. aliens	a. travel	a. singular

Language skills

Fact is something that can be proven. An **opinion** is a feeling or belief that can't be proven.

Now, state whether each of these statements is a fact or opinion.

1. Anansi is a spider. ....
2. Anansi is greedy. ....
3. Turtle is lazy and does not enjoy walking. ....
4. Turtle is clever. ....
5. Anansi is thin. ....
6. Anansi loved the meals that Turtle cooked. ....
7. Turtle lives in the pond. ....
8. This is an interesting story. ....

Write now

Anansi realizes his mistake. He wants to invite Turtle for dinner. Help him write an invitation.

Your invitation must include

- Receiver's name and address (here, the Turtle)
- Date
- Greeting
- Invitation for ....
- Occasion for the invitation
- Additional details—date, time, place
- Complimentary close
- Name

Use phrases like

- I would be delighted/pleased if you ....
- Could you please join us for ....
- We shall look forward to ....
- My family and I shall be waiting ....

Communication corner

A. Listen to a conversation about eating at a restaurant and fill in the blanks.

1. Annie wanted help in locating a restaurant because ....
   a. she wanted to eat something different
   b. she did not know the place
   c. she had lost her way
2. Annie preferred .... food.
   a. North Indian
   b. Italian
   c. French
3. The Italian restaurant was the ....
   a. closest
   b. furthest
   c. difficult to find
4. The Italian restaurant had .... food.
   a. expensive
   b. cheap
   c. unhygienic
5. The Chinese restaurant offered .... food.
6. a. cheap
   b. expensive
   c. spicy
7. The name of the Chinese restaurant was ....
   a. The Dragon
   b. The Chinese
   c. The Pacific

B. Pair up with a friend in class. You two will play the roles of Anansi and Turtle. As Anansi, you have to invite Turtle. Both of you must resolve the issue between you. You could begin by inviting him for dinner. You could accept or refuse the invitation but be kind to each other.

Example: *Accepting*

Anansi: 'I would be happy if you could ...'
Turtle: 'That's very kind of you, thanks.'

Example: *Refusing*

Anansi: 'Would you please join us for dinner on Saturday?'
Turtle: 'That's very kind of you, but actually I'm doing something else on Saturday.'/'I'm really sorry, but I've planned to go away that weekend.'

Worksheet 6

Grammar check

Subject-verb agreement

1. In a sentence, the subject must agree with the verb. If the subject is singular, the verb must also be singular.
2. When the subject of a sentence has two or more nouns or pronouns connected by *and*, use a plural verb. Example: She and her friends go for a walk.
3. When two or more singular nouns or pronouns are connected by *or* or *nor*, use a singular verb. Example: I will either wear a red or a blue dress.
4. The words *each*, *each one, either, neither, everyone, everybody, anybody, anyone, nobody, somebody, someone,* and *no one* are singular and require a singular verb. Example: Nobody knows me here.
5. Nouns that are names of subjects, such as civics, mathematics and news require singular verbs. Example: I love civics.
6. Nouns such as scissors, tweezers, trousers, and shears require plural verbs. (There are two parts to these things.) Example: These trousers are mine.
7. Collective nouns are words that imply more than one person but that are considered singular and take a singular verb, such as group, team, committee, class, and family. Example: The team plays well.

- Singular verb--> The dog chases the cat.
- Plural verb--> The dogs chase the cat.

A. Underline the correct verbs and complete the sentences given below. One has been done for you.

1. The elephants/ ......is...... are ....helping people transport logs.......... .
2. The herd of cattle is/are ....
3. The fairy was/were ....
4. The team of crickters is/are ....

5. A pair of scissors is/are ....
6. The actors was/were ....
7. The horses in the stable was/were ....
8. The lion was/were ....
9. I am/are ....
10. We was/were ....

B. Match the two halves to form correct sentences.

1. The ants	have landed.
2. The aliens	meets after school.
3. My grandfather	needs repair.
4. My teacher	revolves around the earth.
5. My cycle	love sweets.
6. The moon	is a melodious bird.
7. The cuckoo	is an affectionate woman.
8. The doctor	resides at Rashtrapati Bhavan.
9. The quiz club	reaches the hospital at noon.
10. The President of India	reads to me every day.

Now write the subjects and verbs from the sentences in the space below. Also write if they are singular or plural. One has been done for you

Subject	Verb	Singular/plural
1. ants	love	plural

C. **Look at the picture and read the sentences on the next page. Each sentence has an error. Underline the error and write the correct word in the space provided. One has been done for you.**

1. This are Ram Singh's farm. ....is..........
2. He are my neighbour. ....
3. They has a cow. ....
4. It give milk. ....
5. There is many hens on the farm. ....
6. The bullocks ploughs their fields. ....
7. I likes visiting them. ....
8. I plays with their animals. ....

Write now

It's Megan Ant's fifth birthday. Help her write an invitation, inviting her friends to the birthday party. It should look appealing and should have all the correct information.

Remember to put in the following points:

- Name of the addressee
- Date
- Time
- Location
- Directions to the location
- Phone number
- Dress code (if any)
- Theme (if any)
- RSVP note (This is given so that the addressee can let the addresser know if he/she is going to attend the party or not.)

My Computer Ate My Homework

Do you like doing homework? Do you use a computer to do your homework? Has your computer ever behaved badly? Here is a poem about a very badly behaved computer.

My computer ate my homework.
Yes, it's troublesome, but true.
Though it didn't gnaw[1] or nibble[2]
and it didn't chomp or chew.

It digested it completely.
It consumed my homework whole,
when I pressed the Shift and Enter
keys instead of Shift-Control.

It devoured[3] my hours of typing,
every picture, chart and graph,
and it left me most unsettled[4]
when I thought I heard it laugh.

[1]**gnaw:** chew | [2]**nibble:** eat quickly with small bites | [3]**devoured:** ate greedily | [4]**unsettled:** worried

I would guess it was a virus,
or it could have been a worm,
that deleted every bit
but didn't prompt me to confirm.

I suppose I might have pressed Escape
instead of pressing Save,
but, regardless, my computer
now will never misbehave.

For I found a good solution
and I smiled to hear the crash,
when I chucked it out the window
and it landed in the trash.

Kenn Nesbitt

Kenn Nesbitt, Former Children's Poet Laureate (US, 2013-15), is the author of many books for kids, including *Kiss, Kiss Good Night, My Hippo Has the Hiccups, Revenge of the Lunch Ladies,* and many others. His poems have appeared in numerous bestselling anthologies, including every book in the popular *Kids Pick the Funniest Poems* series, and anthologies with nearly two million copies in print. His website, poetry4kids.com, is the most visited children's poetry website on the Internet.

Appreciation

1. Fill the graphic organizer with details from the poem.

Characters: Who are the people?

Setting: Where does it take place?

What is the problem?

How did it happen?

What was the result?

What was the mood of the speaker?

2. Personification is a figure of speech where human qualities are given to animals, objects or ideas. What is personified in this poem? Give an example.

3. A rhyme scheme is the pattern of rhyming words at the end of each line of a poem or song.

   Example:
   Mr Brown, the circus *clown* (a)
   puts his clothes on upside *down*.(a)
   He wears his hat upon his *toes*. (b)
   and socks and shoes upon his *nose*.(b)

   What is the rhyme scheme in this poem?

4. Write a paragraph after reading the following.
   Machines can be very strange at times. One day, cleaning your garage, you find a weird looking machine. You see the buttons and knobs. There you find an 'on' button. You press it and ....

   Begin: 'The moment I pressed the knob, there was a screech! And ...'

Activity

Design a machine that can make your life easier. Keep the following in mind:

- What will it look like? Draw a picture of it.
- Explain what it is supposed to do and how it will work.
- Explain how it has proved to be useful.
- Can you imagine life without it?
- What are the possible disadvantages?

7. Gulliver in the Land Of Giants

Warm-up

In pairs, consider living in a particular fantasy land.

Life situations	Advantages	Disadvantages
a place where all the people are very tiny		
a place where all the people are giants		
a place where you are the only one		

Gulliver was a surgeon who liked to set out on voyages[1]. He had many adventures on these voyages. In the following story, he went on board his small ship, the Adventure, and set out to sail for Surat, in the East Indies. Read on to find out what happened.

[1]**voyages:** a long journey, especially by sea | [2]**furious:** very angry | [3]**blinding:** making it difficult to see

We left the Cape of Good Hope and sailed through the Straits of Madagascar on our way to India. There, the south-west monsoon wind sprang up. This wind was furious[2] and the rain fell in blinding[3] sheets.

Luckily, we saw land. We sailed towards it and cast anchor[4]. The sailors walked along the beach looking for fresh water. I walked up the hill, hoping to see people or houses, from the top. I saw the country was rocky and bare, without trees or grass. Soon I was weary, and turned back towards the ship.

I was horrified to see the crew rowing away anxiously. They were being followed by an enormous man, bigger than a giant!

I turned and ran for my life. I scrambled up a steep hill. To my great surprise, I saw cultivated fields of huge sizes. The grass in them was twenty feet high. I also noticed that crop rose up forty feet like tall trees. Suddenly, a monstrous man strode towards me. I ran to hide in the corn. He called out in a gruff[5], roaring voice, that filled the air like thunder.

At this several other great men came there, carrying a gigantic[6] reaping hook[7]. I crouched[8] close to the ground, but a giant picked me up in his palm at a height of nearly sixty feet from the ground. I knew it was useless to struggle. If I slipped through his fingers, I would die.

The giant seemed to be pleased. Holding me in his palm, the giant ran to his master, the farmer.

The farmer and his men watched my movements with fascination[9]. The farmer, then, carried me home.

'See what I've brought!' said he to his wife.

They sat around the table and laughed so loud that my ears rang with the sound. After dinner, they put me on a bed that was nearly sixty feet wide and over twenty feet from the floor. I slept because I was very tired.

The next morning, the farmer's young daughter stitched clothes for me and played with me. From her, I quickly learnt their language. I called her 'Glumdalclitch', which in their country means 'little nurse'. I learnt I was in a country called Brobdingnag.

The farmer thought, 'Here is my chance to make money. I'll take this little creature to the market and make each person pay to look at him.'

[4] **cast anchor:** to drop or let go an anchor to keep a ship at rest | [5]**gruff:** deep and rough, and often sounding unfriendly; [6]**gigantic:** very huge | [7]**reaping hook:** a sickle | [8]**crouched:** bend down | [9]**fascination:** the state of being very interested in somebody/something

The next day, the farmer carried me with him, in a box that had a little door and holes for air. People came from hundreds of miles. They were fascinated with a tiny human being who could speak and perform a hundred funny tricks. I didn't like being treated like a monkey. Moreover, I grew tired because the work was tedious[10] and the room, crowded.

One day, the Queen of the country heard of me and summoned the farmer. She was charmed by my manners and paid a thousand gold pieces and bought me. She also asked Glumdalclitch to stay in the palace to take care of me.

I was a favourite of the Royal Family. The Queen's cabinet-maker made me a beautiful box with a bed, some chairs, a table, and a little cabinet for my clothes. I was so well looked after and quickly regained my health.

[10]**tedious:** taking too long and not interesting

Here, I had some misadventures too! One morning, Glumdalclitch put my box on the window-sill for fresh air. The door and windows of my room were open. And it happened that on a plate on my table, there was a piece of sweet cake. This attracted wasps, as big as partridges. They were humming louder than bagpipes. I was terrified and had to fight them with my sword.

One day, the Queen thought I would enjoy a little rowing exercise. Soon, a boat suitable to my size was made. It was fitted with mast and sail. It was then, set in a trough[11] of water. I used to row daily. The Queen and the ladies of the Court were happy watching me.

But here, too, I had an accident. Once, when one of the Court pages[12], while filling the trough, poured in with one of the buckets of water, a large frog. The animal climbed up over one side of the boat. It jumped over me and almost suffocated me. But I hit it with an oar till it jumped overboard.

[11]**trough:** a long narrow open container for animals to eat or drink from | [12]**pages:** young attendants

But my narrowest of all my escapes was from a monkey. Glumdalclitch had left me in her room. I saw a monkey as bulky as an elephant come through the window. I saw it tear everything to pieces. At last it came and peeped into my box. I tried to hide, but it snatched me. Then, strangely, it began to gently stroke me. Just then, the door opened and Glumdalclitch came in. The monkey heard the noise and at once, jumped out of the window, carrying me with it. Glumdalclitch screamed so much that soon a crowd gathered.

Meanwhile, the animal fled to the roof. It sat there stuffing my mouth with nuts. At this, the crowd in the courtyard shrieked with laughter. Soon ladders were got. As soon as the monkey saw that it was likely to be caught, it dropped me and fled. One man climbed up and got me down safely.

I stayed on in Brobdingnag for two years but longed to go back to England. And at last I got freedom from my bondage[13]!

[13]**bondage:** the state of being a slave or prisoner

The King and Queen journeyed to the south coast of the country. Glumdalclitch and I were taken along. I was carried in my box. Although it was comfortable, but at the end of the journey I had fever. Glumdalclitch felt that fresh air would do me good. So she handed my box to a boy to carry me to the shore for fresh air.

There I sat, in the box, gazing at the sea till I fell asleep. I was awakened by a violent jerk at my box. I knew I was being carried through the air. From the window, I could see nothing but clouds.

Overhead, I could hear a sound of the beat of wings. I guessed that a huge eagle had swooped down and picked up my box. And suddenly I felt myself falling down. After a minute, my box was floating in the sea.

I slid open the roof and shouted, 'Help!'

'Ahoy!' roared a voice. It was a joyful sound. 'You are quite safe, and alongside a British ship,' said the voice and pulled me into the ship.

I told them my story. They stared with disbelief. But I showed them various things that I had—the huge comb, foot-long pins, and the Queen's gold ring which I wore in my neck.

The ship reached England. To me the people looked so small. And for many months, I feared getting crushed under people's feet!

Adapted from 'Gulliver's Travels' by Jonathan Swift

Jonathan Swift (1667 –1745) was an Irish author who wrote novels, essays and political pamphlets. He was also a poet and a priest. He is remembered for works such as Gulliver's Travels (the original name of the book was *Travels into Several Remote Nations of the World. In Four Parts. By Lemuel Gulliver, First a Surgeon, and then a Captain of Several Ships), The Battle of the Books and A Tale of a Tub*. He originally published all of his works under pseudonyms – such as Lemuel Gulliver, Isaac Bickerstaff, MB Drapier – or anonymously.

Read and answer

1. What natural disaster struck *The Adventure* after they crossed the Straits?
2. What did Gulliver notice about the place where they haboured their ship?
3. What made the crew sail away in a hurry?
4. Mention five things in the strange land that tell you that Gulliver was in the land of giants.
5. What did Gulliver name the farmer's daughter? Why did he give her that name?
6. Why does Gulliver feel that he was liked at the palace?
7. *But here, too, I had an accident.*
   a. Who is the 'I'?
   b. Where is he/she? How did he/she get there?
   c. What is the 'accident' being spoken of?
8. Complete the columns to explain the misadventures Gulliver has and how he is saved.

	What was the misadventure?	What saved him?
a.		
b.		
c.		

d. [ ] → [ ]

9. How did Gulliver prove to the Captain that the land of giants did exist?

Think and answer

1. What, according to you, was the worst misadventure Gulliver had? Why do you think so?
2. The farmer was a greedy man and an unfeeling man? Do you agree/ disagree? Why?
3. Imagine you are Gulliver. Write a letter to your friend, describing your best experience.
4. Would you like to visit a land as strange as Brobdingnag? Why?
5. Gulliver was very well looked after, yet he longed to go back to England. Why?
6. One day, after a plane crash, you find yourself in the land of giants. You are rescued after a day. Describe the experience.

VB

Word power

What words in the story mean the words in bold italics? The first letter has been given to you.

1. The citizens were ***terrified*** by the bombings. h ....
2. Anna looked at the paper ***nervously***. a ....
3. The people in the land were ***enormous***. g ....
4. The child looked at the plane with ***interest***. f ....
5. The judged ***sent for*** the accused. s ....
6. The shipwrecked crew suffered a great deal of ***misfortune***. m ....
7. All of us slept after a ***tiresome*** journey. t ....
8. The hero freed the people from ***oppression***. b ....

Grammar check

Modal verbs

Read the following sentences.

We usually don't speak the same way to all the people we meet. We speak more formally to strangers and more politely to people who are older to us. We speak in a more informal way with our friends, people we know very well, as well as with those who are younger than us.

To speak in a formal or informal way or to ask permission, we often use verbs called *modals verbs.*

> A **modal verb** is a special type of helping verb. Some modal verbs are: may, could, can, shall, should, would, etc.

These verbs help us to be polite and respectful towards people.

We use *may* to ask polite permission or give polite answers.

We use *can* or *could* to ask permission or to give permission.

Choose the correct modals from the brackets to fill in the blanks.

1. You (might/could) .... wear my dress for the party.
2. .... (Could/May) you please, open the wardrobe?
3. .... (May/Can) you please give me your notebook?
4. Do you know if the teacher .... (may/can) meet us today?
5. I'm sorry but you .... (cannot/may not) take my books without my permission.
6. (Can/May) .... you help the baby pack his bag?
7. (Would/May) .... I sit beside you, please?
8. (Could/May) .... you please play the flute for me?

Language skills

A word that is made by joining two words is called a **compound word**.

Examples: day + light = daylight
country + side = countryside
card + board = cardboard

Combine the words from the two sets below to form compound words. Then use them in sentences.

kind	rain	arm	door	lamp
foot	ever	snow	key	day

chair	print	post	hole	green
knob	dream	hearted	fall	flakes

Write now

Informal letter

Informal letters are the ones that we write to friends and relatives. They are informal because we are communicating with people who are close to us. The style of writing can be relaxed.

Look at the format below:

Sender's address (without name) →	Flat No. 2, L2 199D Kalkaji, New Delhi 110019
Date →	17 January 2017
Salutation →	Dear Manu
Message →	[.......... ....]
Subscription →	Yours affectionately,
Signature →	Tia

A letter can be divided into a number of parts.

1. The *heading* (writer's address, date), which is written on the left hand side of the page.
2. The *greeting* with which you begin the letter:
   This depends on the relation between you and the person to whom you are writing.
   Informal letters may begin like this: *My dear Granny*, *Dear Shyam,* etc.
3. The *communication* or *message*, which is also called the body of the letter:
   Write it neatly. Divide your letter into paragraphs. Use simple language.
4. The *conclusion* or the *subscription* is a very important part of a letter. You cannot end the letter suddenly by just signing your name. That would be rude. You have to end the letter politely.
   Informal letters may be ended like this: *Your loving friend*, *Your loving son* (or *daughter/nephew/niece* and so on), *Yours affectionately*. This subscription may be written on the left hand side of the page. The first word of the subscription always begins with a capital letter.
5. The *signature* or the writer's name comes just below the subscription.

Gulliver is very grateful to be back in England. As Gulliver, write a letter to a friend telling him/her about your escape from Brobdingnag.

Communication corner

A. Listen to a description of another fantasy creature. His name is Gollum and he is a character from *The Hobbit,* by J. R. R. Tolkein. Fill in the blanks given below by ticking the correct option.

1. Gollum was a .... creature. (thin/normal/plump)
2. He lived .... (on the mountains/in the lake/on misty lands).
3. Gollum had a .... complexion. (dark/pale/fair)
4. He had big eyes because he was always trying to peep through dark .... (earth/tunnels/water).
5. Gollum lived alone. Hence spoke to .... (fishes/devils/himself).
6. Gollum had a peculiar way of boating. It was the habit of .... (gurgling/coughing/rowing very quietly).
7. Gollum loved eating .... (birds/fish/plants).
8. Gollum's treasure was his .... of invisibility. (ring/gold coin/wealth)

B. Divide yourselves into groups. Each group must enact one of these scenes. You must suggest solutions to each of these problems.

- You and your friends see Gollum try to catch his dinner from the lake. But he is unable to. He is feeling upset. Do you help?
- You find Gollum in a situation where others are making fun of him because he is different from everyone else.
- You find Gollum's ring but he doesn't know it.
- You try on the ring and play tricks on Gollum and your friends.

Worksheet 7

Grammar check

Modal verbs

We use modal verbs to show if we believe something is certain, probable or possible (or not). We also use modals to talk about ability, to ask permission, to make requests and offers and so on.

Rules of usage:

1. We use modals when we are sure that something has happened/is happening/will happen.
   Example: I just boiled water, it must be very hot.
2. We use 'can' and 'could' to talk about an ability to do something.
   Example: She can dance well.
3. We can use verbs such as 'must' or 'should' to say when something is necessary or unnecessary, or to give advice.
   Example: It's sweltering, we must carry umbrellas.
4. We can use verbs such as 'can', 'could' and 'may' to ask for and give permission. We also use modal verbs to say that something is not allowed.
   Example: Can I borrow your book , please?
5. We can use 'will' and 'would' to talk about habits or things we usually do or did.
   Example: I will be there on time.

A. Write questions using the words in brackets. Write answers that are true about you.

Example: Can you read and write English?
Yes, I can/No, I can't.

1. .... (ride bicycle)
   ....
2. .... (cook dinner)
   ....
3. .... (swim)
   ....

4. .... (play golf)

....

5. .... (dance on stage)

....

6. .... (fly a kite)

....

7. .... (knit a sweater)

....

8. .... (change a tyre)

....

B. Fill in the blanks with the words given below.

can	could	may	must

1. I .... ride a bicycle when I was 4 years old.
2. .... we go out for dinner?
3. We .... always tell the truth.
4. It .... rain today.
5. I .... read this book if I have the time.
6. We .... help the poor and needy.
7. We .... all draw and paint.
8. Shweta .... speak in many languages.
9. I .... reach the station on time.
10. Robin .... play the trombone.

C. Choose the most appropriate modals to express what has been mentioned in each bracket.

1. .... I speak to the Managing Director, please? I need to discuss an important issue. (a formal polite request)

   a. Can b. May c. Must d. Could

2. .... give me your notebook for the day? (a polite request)

   a. Could you b. Must you c. Would you d. May you

3. .... if I join your game ? (asking permission)

a. Must you mind   b. Can you let   c. What   d. Would you mind

4. .... you help me with my project work, please? (Informal request)

a. Can   b. Can't   c. Must   d. Why don't you

5. Would you mind if I .... your pen? (polite request)

a. will borrow   b. can borrowed   c. must borrow   d. could borrow

6. Could I talk to you for a minute? Yes, you .... (permission given)

a. could   b. can   c. will   d. must

7. Could you give me a lift home, please? I'm sorry, I .... I'm not going that way. (permission not given)

a. can't   b. won't   c. mustn't   d. couldn't

D. Complete this list of Dos and Don'ts for your school notice board. Use only *must/should*.

Dos and Don'ts

1. We should reach the school on time.
2. We must not shout at each other.
3. ....
4. ....
5. ....
6. ....
7. ....
8. ....
9. ....
10. ....

Write now

You have just had an unusual experience which you find hard to rationalize. Write a letter to your cousin to tell him about it. Remember to format the letter correctly.

8. Too Many Professors

Warm-up

1. **If you could invent one thing, what would it be?**
2. **How would it help you, your school and your community? Fill in the table below.**

You	School	Community

Now read about a professor who invented a very unique potion.

Professor Branestawm loves inventing. But unfortunately all his inventions land him in the worst possible situations. Sometimes even his housekeeper, Mrs Flittersnoop, and his best friend, Colonel Dedshott, also get caught with him in the trouble.

[1]**larder:** a cupboard/ closet used for storing food

[2]**resound:** to fill a place with sound | [3]**odour:** smell

It's only getting wet! Very good, sir. And now I must be getting back to my cakes.
Wait! It takes time. Look, look!
Oo-er! It's going all lumpy! Apples coming alive!
Except for a little papery flavour, the apples are certainly a success. Now, I shall spray a picture of a box of chocolates. But sadly, it costs more to make the liquid than it would cost to buy the things.
You don't say! I'll enjoy those chocolates.
There are certain limitations to the power of the liquid. The things it brings to life go back as they were when the liquid dries off.
I don't know yet, whether it will work with animals or people.

Meow!
Amazing! O god the elephant too!
I'm leaving! I'll be with my sister, Aggie, today!
Oh God! The silly elephant has dropped the entire liquid on my photograph album.
Heavens! I'll dry the elephant. It will make it go back into a picture.

All the photographs in the album had come alive. There were many Professors at various ages, numerous Flittersnoops and all the other people that had been photographed once upon a time.

Terrible! Terrible! The poor policeman! Only half of him was captured in the camera.
Pass please.
Oh dear! What if I get mixed up with all these come-to-life photo sort of people and forget which is really me? Oh God! The door bell ringing too!
Ha! Hullo, Branestawm!
Party on! Sorry to intrude. WHAT!!! Been for a holiday? You're looking well, and ten years younger.

[4]**imposter:** a person who pretends to be somebody else in order to trick people | [5]**routed:** a situation in which somebody is defeated easily and completely in a battle or competition

Norman Hunter

Norman George Lorimer Hunter (1899-1995) was a children's author from Great Britain. He is best known for creating Professor Branestawm. The Branestawm series was originally meant for the radio. The first illustrated book was published in 1933 and the second one in 1937. Hunter is also known for writing on advertising and conjuring, among other things.

Read and answer

1. Fill in the story mountain.

The problem becomes worse when:

....

....

The problem starts when:

....

....

....

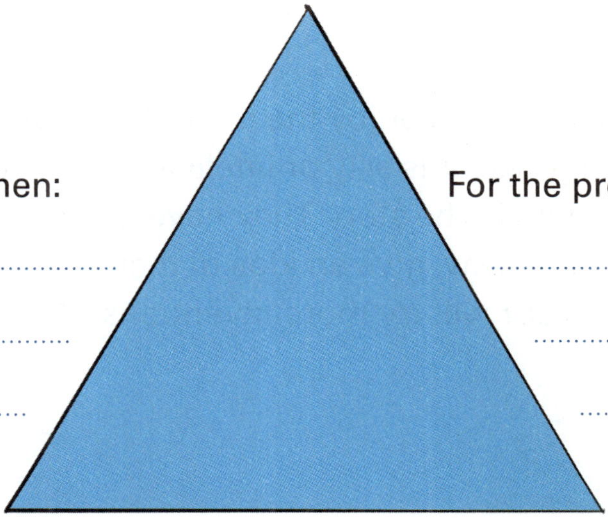

For the problem to improve:

....

....

....

Beginning: ....

....

....

Ending: ....

....

....

2. How did Mrs Flittersnoop realize that something was wrong? What did she think it was? What was the truth?

3. Mrs Flittersnoop's reaction changed when more and more things came to life. Fill in the table with information from the text.

Invention	Mrs Flittersnoop's reaction
a. apples	
b. chocolates	

c. elephant

4. What is Colonel's first reaction to Professor? How does the reaction change?

Think and answer

1. Which part of the story did you enjoy the most? What did you like about it?
2. Do you think that the Professor is silly or intelligent? Why do you think so? VB
3. There are three characters in the story. They have peculiar names. Do you think their names in some way, give an idea of their personality? Explain. VB
4. Do you think the Professor will try more inventions? Yes/No? Why do you think so?

Word power

What do the words in the story mean? Circle the correct answer.

1. Whatever can that awful smell be?
   a. terrible b. poor c. frightful d. shocking
2. Amazing! Astounding ! Come to my study, Mrs Flittersnoop.
   a. never before b. funny c. surprising d. intelligent
3. The terrible odour!
   a. smell b. taste c. perfume d. colour
4. There are certain limitations to the power of the liquid.
   a. minimum b. greatest c. height d. boundaries
5. The poor policeman! Only half of him was captured in the camera.
   a. inside b. described c. shown d. detain
6. Impostor, scoundrel! That is not me at all, I'm me here.
   a. cheat b. devil c. liar d. funny

Grammar check

Adverbs of degree

Read these sentences.

Mrs Flittersnoop was *extremely* scared.
Seeing the doubles, Col.? Dedshott was *greatly* confused.
The professor was *very* excited with his new invention.

Adverbs of degree tell us the strength of something that happens. They answer the question that asks *How much?* or *How little?*

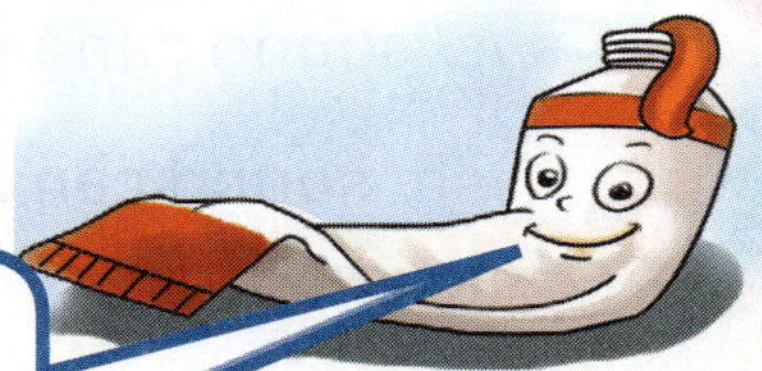

Adverbs of degree include: sufficiently, almost, entirely, extremely, greatly, highly, hugely, immensely, moderately, partially, perfectly, practically, strongly, totally, very, etc.

Tick the correct word.

1. The water was *entirely/extremely* cold.
2. The book is *greatly/quite* exciting.
3. He was *just/almost* leaving.
4. I had *sufficiently/almost* finished.
5. The situation was *very/greatly* serious.
6. My teacher is *extremely/entirely* kind.
7. My sister is *much/hugely* older than me.
8. I travelled to *many/almost* new countries.

Pronunciation

Some consonant sounds can be spelled in more than one way.

'sh' as in shoes, shopping, sugar

's' as in sooner, said, science

A. Place the following words in the correct columns.

fish silent brush sea shirt straw cash sheep socks slow soft

'sh' sound	's' sound

B. Now repeat these tongue twisters to practice *sh* and *s* sound.

1. She sells seashells on a seashore. The shells she sells are seashells, I'm sure
2. Sally's shop stocks short spotted socks.

Interestingly enough, the *s* and *sh* sounds can be achieved by other letters too.

/s/ sound can be made by *s* and *c*. Examples: sign, centre

/sh/ sound can be made by *sh, ch, ci* and *ti*. Examples: ship, chef, special, action

C. Correct the spellings given below.

sertify	cervise	petishun	nayshun	shampagne	mashine	sentipede
sircle	caid	mencion	musitian	inichial	cecshun	ctar

Write now

Kid-powered inventions

In 1858, a 15-year-old boy, named Chester Greenwood, invented earmuffs. He wanted to keep his ears warm during bitter winters. He made 2 ear-shaped loops from wire, and asked his grandmother to sew fur on them. He made a fortune selling them to soldiers during World War I. There are many such smart kids who invented something.

If you could think of any invention to change the world, and make it a better place, what would you invent?

Describe the object. You must mention:

- Dimensions—shape, colour, design, material
- Purpose/use
- Functions/importance
- Price
- Availability
- Summing up

Communication corner

A. Listen to a poem, *Mr Brown the Circus Clown* by Kenn Nesbitt. Then fill in the table given below.

Mr Brown wears various things incorrectly. What are these?

1. clothes	
2. hat	
3. shoes	
4. tie	
5. earrings	
6. stockings	
7. shirt and coat	

B. Pick a partner and play the parts of Mr Brown and a school student. Imagine that you see Mr Brown on the street. Have a conversation with him.

You could talk about:

- How surprised you are
- Why he is dressed like that
- What he does all day
- Talk about yourself a little

Worksheet 8

Grammar check

Adverbs of degree

Adverbs of degree describe to what degree, level or extent something is done. In other words, they answer *how much* or to *what degree.* They are used to add more information to verbs, adjectives and other adverbs.

- almost
- nearly
- quite
- just
- too
- enough
- hardly
- scarcely
- completely
- very
- extremely

A. Fill in the blanks with suitable adverbs from the box. The same adverb can be used more than once.

occasionally	sometimes	usually	rarely	once
very	never	mostly	often	always

1. I .... go to bed at 10 o'clock.
2. I have .... been to the USA.
3. I have been to Australia just ....
4. I .... take a bath before I go to bed.
5. My grandparents live in Kerala. I visit them ....
6. My friends are .... vegetarians.

7. I was .... impressed with her performance.
8. I .... go for a walk in the park.
9. I watch English films ....
10. They .... go out.

B. There is a mistake in each line given below. Write down the mistake and the correct answer in the space provided. One has been done for you.

	Mistake	Correction
1. Maya is extreme happy because she won the race.	extreme	extremely
2. Jayant had completely forgot.	....	....
3. Sharon often come late to work.	....	....
4. I arrived quiet late to the party.	....	....
5. Rohan danced very good in the programme.	....	....
6. You can hard see the dent on the car.	....	....
7. We got just enuf sleep before the trek at 5 a.m.	....	....
8. Sometime I like to sing in the bathroom.	....	....
9. Divya has ever been to Paris.	....	....
10. They were two excited to sleep before the match.	....	....

C. Rewrite the following sentences after adding a suitable adverb. In some cases, the meaning of the sentences may change. DO NOT repeat the adverbs.

1. The music is loud.

   ....

2. The mangoes are ripe.

   ....

3. My teacher is kind.

   ....

   ....

4. I take this route to school.

   ....

   ....

5. Janvi is helpful.

   ....

6. I have finished my homework.

....

7. Ants are small.

....

8. Rehan is busy these days.

....

....

9. Romila forgot to do her homework.

....

....

10. Tarun missed the schoolbus.

....

....

D. Fill in the blanks with the adverbs given below.

really   absolutely   pretty   highly   rather   remarkably   fairly   completely

1. She was .... exhausted by the end of the day.
2. My friend is .... nice.
3. It was a .... scary place.
4. It was a .... simple problem.
5. I write .... well.
6. The magic show was .... amazing.
7. My father is a .... skilled surgeon.
8. The building is .... high.

Write now

You are a detective. In the search of a painting which was stolen from a museum, you have entered an abandoned warehouse. Inside you discover a strange machine. Describe the machine. What does it do? What do you do with it? Does it help you? Be creative and provide the relevant details.

....

....

The Little Big Man

How often do you wish you were a grown-up? Why do you want to be a grown-up? Do you think it is fun? Here is a poem about a boy who wants to be a grown-up as soon as possible.

I am small because I am a little child. I shall be big when I am as old as my father is.

My teacher will come and say, 'It is late, bring your slate[1] and your books.'

I shall tell him, 'Do you not know I am as big as father? And I must not have lessons any more.'

My master will wonder and say, 'He can leave his books if he likes, for he is grown up.'

I shall dress myself and walk to the fair where the crowd is thick.

My uncle will come rushing up to me and say, 'You will get lost, my boy; let me carry you.'

I shall answer, 'Can't you see, uncle, I am as big as father. I must go to the fair alone.'

Uncle will say, 'Yes, he can go wherever he likes, for he is grown up.'

Mother will come from her bath when I am giving money to my nurse, for I shall know how to open the box with my key.

Mother will say, 'What are you about, naughty child?'

[1]**slate:** (here) a small sheet of a type of dark grey stone in a wooden frame, used in the past in schools, for children to write on

I shall tell her, 'Mother, don't you know, I am as big as father, and I must give silver to my nurse.'

Mother will say to herself, 'He can give money to whom he likes, for he is grown up.'

In the holiday time in October father will come home and, thinking that I am still a baby, will bring for me from the town little shoes and small silken frocks.

I shall say, 'Father, give them to my *dada*[2],' for I am as big as you are.'

Father will think and say, 'He can buy his own clothes if he likes, for he is grown up.'

Rabindranath Tagore

[2]**dada:** brother (in Bengali)

Rabindranath Tagore (1861 –1941) was a Bengali poet, author, songwriter and playwright who reshaped Bengali literature and music, as well as Indian art in 19th and early 20th centuries. He wrote *Gitanjali* and the songs in the *Gitobitan.* His works introduced the best of Indian culture to the West and vice versa. He became the first non-European to win the Nobel Prize in Literature in 1913.

Appreciation

1. The young boy imagines his life when he grows up. Fill in the table to bring out the life that he dreams about.

	What will they say?	What will the boy answer?
a. Teacher		
b. Uncle		
c. Mother		
d. Father		

2. Why is the name of the poem *The Little Big Man*?
3. How old do you think is the speaker of the poem? Why do you think so?
4. What are the things that you are not allowed to do because you are too young? Are all children spoken to, in this way by the adults? Give two more examples.
5. Why do you think do elders not let you do certain things? How do you feel about it? VB
6. What is the tone of the speaker: sad, happy, longing or horrified? Why do you think so?
7. This poem is written like ordinary speech. Do you like this pattern of writing a poem?
8. Write a stanza about what you would like to do when you grow up. VB

Activity

Fill in the Venn diagram to compare and contrast your life now and when you grow up. Then write a couple of short paragraphs. Begin: I'd rather be ...

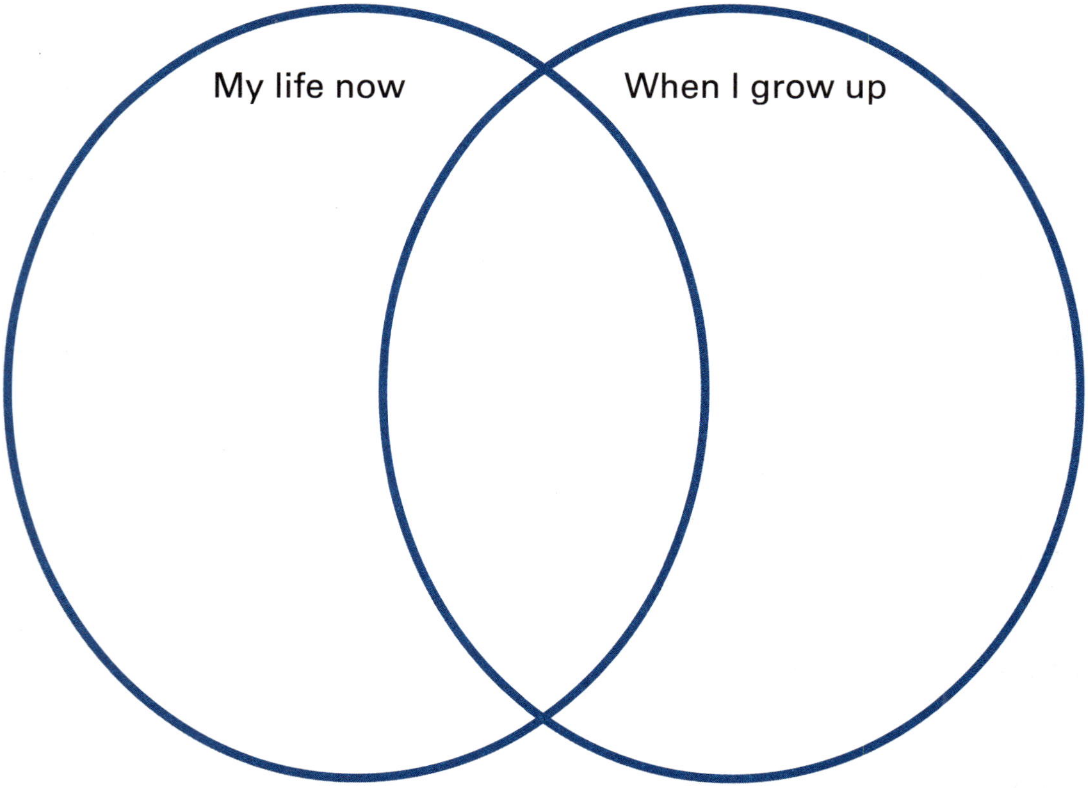

9. How the First Letter was Written

Warm-up

In pre-historic times, before we had the alphabet, people communicated through pictures. In fact, one of the most famous forms of pictorial writing was the Egyptian hieroglyphs, which can still be seen today on the walls of the pyramids.

Look at the photograph given below. This form of communication existed even before the hieroglyphs.

Write a message to your friend using only pictures. Be sure to exchange your work with your classmate and ask them to figure out what the message is. Be creative and smart.

Now read about a little girl and the message she drew for her mother.

Characters

Narrator

Tegumai—a young man

Teshumai—Tegumai's wife

Taffy—Tegumai and Teshumai's daughter

Stranger-man

Head Chief

Many tribal men and women

Scene I

Narrator: It happened long ago when people lived in caves. One day, Tegumai and Taffy go fishing through beaver[1]-swamp[2] to the Wagai river to catch fish for dinner. Tegumai's spear is made of wood with shark's teeth at the end. Before he can catch any fish, tragedy strikes. The spear breaks.

Tegumai: This is bad luck, Taffy. We are miles away from home and I have forgotten to bring any extra spears. It will take me half the day to mend this.

Taffy: There's your big black spear at home. Let me run back to the cave and bring it.

Tegumai: It's too far for your little legs. Besides, you might fall into the beaver-swamp and be drowned. I will try to mend the spear.

Taffy: (*sitting with her toes in the water*) Daddy, it's an awful nuisance[3] that you and I don't know how to write, isn't it? If we did, we could send a message for the new spear.

[1]**beaver:** a fur-coated animal that lives on land and in water |
[2]**swamp:** soft wet land (A beaver-swamp is a swamp full of beavers.) |
[3]**nuisance:** a situation that is annoying or causes trouble or problems

Narrator: Just then a Stranger-man came along the river, but he belonged to another tribe and did not understand Tegumai's language. He stood on the bank and smiled at Taffy, because he had a little daughter of his own, at home.

Taffy: (*to the stranger*) Come here. Do you know where my Mummy lives?

Stranger-man: Urn!

Taffy: Daddy, look at that shoal of fish! It's sad that you can't use your spear.

Tegumai: (*mending his spear and not looking at the stranger*) Don't bother grown-ups, Taffy.

Taffy: (*stamping her foot*) I only want him to go to our home and get a spear and he won't understand.

Stranger-man: (*to himself*) This is a very wonderful child. She stamps her foot at me and makes faces. She must be the daughter of that noble Chief who is so great that he won't take any notice of me.

Taffy: I want you to go to my Mummy, because your legs are longer than mine, and you won't fall into the beaver-swamp, and ask for Daddy's other spear, the one with the black handle that hangs over our fireplace.

Stranger-man: (*to himself*) This truly is a wonderful child. She waves her arms and shouts at me, but I don't understand a word of what she says. But if I don't do what she wants, I greatly fear the haughty[4] Chief will be angry.

[4]**haughty:** behaving in an unfriendly way towards other people because you think that you are better than them

Narrator: Stranger-man got up and twisted a big flat piece of bark off a birch-tree and gave it to Taffy. He did this to show that his heart was as white as the birch-bark and that he meant no harm.

Taffy: Oh! You want my Mummy's address? Of course I can't write, but I can draw pictures if I've anything sharp to scratch with. Please lend me the shark's tooth off your necklace.

Narrator: The Stranger-man didn't say anything, so Taffy put up her little hand and pulled at the beautiful shark-tooth necklace round his neck. Then she lay down flat on her tummy with her legs in the air and began to draw.

Taffy: Now I'll draw a message. First I'll draw Daddy fishing. It isn't very like him; but Mummy will know. I've drawn his spear all broken. Now I'll draw the other spear that he wants. It looks as if it was sticking in Daddy's back, but that's because the shark's tooth slipped and this piece of bark isn't big enough. That's the spear I want you to fetch and this is me. My hair doesn't stand up like I've drawn, but it's easier to draw that way. Now I'll draw you. I think you're very nice really, but I can't make you pretty in the picture, so you mustn't be offended. Are you offended?

Narrator: The Stranger-man only smiled and smiled.

Taffy: Look, now I've drawn you, and I've put the spear that Daddy wants into your hand, just to remind you that you're to bring it. Now I'll draw the way home. You go along till you come to two trees and then you go over a hill and then you come into a beaver-swamp, all full of beavers. Mind you don't fall in! Then our cave is just beyond the beaver-swamp. That's my Mummy outside. Now, in case you forget, I've drawn the spear that Daddy wants. You show the picture to my Mummy and she'll give it to you. Isn't it a beautiful picture? And do you quite understand, or shall I explain again?

Narrator: The Stranger-man looked at the picture and nodded very hard.

Tegumai: What have you been doing, Taffy? See I have mended my spear and I'm going fishing.

Scene II

Narrator: The Stranger-man hurried away with the picture and ran for some miles, till quite by accident he found Teshumai at the door of her cave, talking to some other ladies who had come to lunch. The Stranger-man handed Teshumai the drawing. As soon as Teshumai saw the picture she screamed and attacked the Stranger-man. The other ladies immediately knocked him down and sat on him in a long line of six, while Teshumai pulled his hair.

Teshumai: This man has struck my Tegumai. See Tegumai all full of spears, and poor Taffy is so frightened that her hair stands on end. And now he has got for me this horrid picture of how it was done. Look!

(*showing picture to all the ladies sitting on the Stranger-man*)

Here is my Tegumai with his arm broken; here is the spear sticking into his back and here is another man throwing a spear from a cave, and here are a whole pack of people.

Narrator: The people were actually Taffy's beavers, but they did look rather like people.

Ladies: *(filling Stranger-man's hair with mud)* Most shocking!

Scene III

Narrator: By this time the Stranger-man was really annoyed. They had filled his hair quite solid with mud, they had rolled him up and down on pebbles, they had sat upon him and had thumped[5] him till he could hardly breathe. Stanger-man understood nothing but led the ladies back to the bank of the Wagai river. The women saw Taffy making daisy-chains and Tegumai fishing.

Taffy: Well, you *have* been quick! But why did you bring so many people? Daddy dear, aren't you surprised?

[5]**thumped:** to hit hard, especially with a closed hand

Tegumai: Very. But why is the entire tribe here?

Teshumai: (*kissing Taffy*) I'm so happy that you are alright.

Head Chief: (*shaking Tegumai severely*) You are alright.

People of the tribe: Explain! Explain! Explain!

Tegumai: Goodness! I broke my spear and the whole countryside turned up?

Taffy: And you've not brought my Daddy's spear! And what are you doing to my nice Stranger-man?

Teshumai: Where are the bad people who speared you, my darling?

Tegumai: There are no bad people. My only visitor this morning was the good man.

Head Chief: He came with a horrible picture that showed you were full of spears.

Taffy: (*unhappily*) I think I'll explain that picture.

Head Chief: Explain! Explain! Explain!

Taffy: I wanted the Stranger-man to fetch Daddy's spear, so I drew a picture. There was only one spear. I drew it three times to make sure. I couldn't help it looking as if it stuck into Daddy's head. And those things that Mummy called bad people are my beavers. I drew them to show him the way through the swamp; and I drew Mummy at the mouth of the cave looking pleased because he is a nice Stranger-man. Why have you filled his hair with mud?

Narrator: Nobody said anything at all for a long time, till the Head Chief laughed; then the Stranger-man laughed; then Tegumai laughed till he fell down flat on the bank; then all the tribe laughed more and louder.

Head Chief: O! You've hit upon a great invention.

Taffy: I only wanted Daddy's spear.

Head Chief: Never mind. It is a great invention and some day men will call it writing. At present it is only pictures but a time will come when we shall make letters—all twenty-six of them. Then we shall always say exactly what we mean without any mistakes.

Narrator: The tribe thanked the Stranger-man. But from that day on, most little girls have liked to draw pictures.

Adapted and abridged from 'Just So Stories' by Rudyard Kipling

Joseph Rudyard Kipling (1865 –1936) was an English journalist, short-story writer, poet, and novelist. Kipling was one of the most popular writers in the United Kingdom, in both prose and verse, in the late 19th and early 20th centuries. Some of his most famous works of fiction include *The Jungle Book* (1894), *Kim* (1901), and many short stories. Some of his famous poems are *Mandalay* (1890), *Gunga Din* (1890), and *If—* (1910). He is considered to be a major innovator in the art of the short stories. He was awarded the Nobel Prize in Literature in 1907. He was the first English-language writer to receive the prize, and its youngest recipient to date. He was also considered for a knighthood and the British Poet Laureateship but he declined both.

Read and answer

1. Where were Taffy and her father? Why did they go there?
2. *This is a very wonderful child. She stamps her foot at me and makes faces.*
   a. Who is the speaker? Who is she/he talking about? Where are they?
   b. Why is 'she' stamping her foot and making faces?
   c. Was the speaker afraid? If so, why?
3. Why did Stranger-man give Taffy the bark? What did Taffy do with it?
4. Who was Stranger-man? Why did he agree to take the message to Tegumai's wife?
5 *Now I'll draw a message.*
   a. Who wrote the message? What did the message say?
   b. Describe the message.
   c. Did Stranger-man manage to deliver the message?
   d. What reception did Stranger-man meet with at Tegumai's house?

Think and answer

1. Taffy's message was the cause of the confusion. Fill in the table to show what Taffy had drawn and how was it interpreted.

What Taffy had drawn	How it was interpreted
a. a broken spear and one that Tegumai wanted	a. Sticking to Tegumai's back. The women felt Tegumai was being attacked.

2. What kind of a girl was Taffy? Pick words that describe her and give a reason for each of the qualities.

haughty   concerned   intelligent   inventive   lazy   loving

3. Which character do you like best in the story? Why?
4. Do you think life was tougher when man had not made many inventions? Give three examples to support your answer.

Word power

Idioms

An **idiom** is a group of words or a fixed expression that has a figurative, or sometimes literal, meaning. The meaning is usually different from the meanings of the individual words.

Match the animal idioms to their meanings.

Idiom	Meaning
1. raining cats and dogs	be patient
2. bull in a china shop	very tired
3. early bird catches the worm	to be uncomfortable in some situation
4. hold your horses	to surprise everyone
5. fish out of water	raining heavily
6. to be dog tired	a person who upsets things or plans
7. to pull a rabbit out of the hat	to get the largest advantage
8. to get a lion's share	if you do think on time, you stand to benefit

Grammar check

Conjunctions

Read these sentences.

We are miles away from home *and* I have forgotten to bring any extra spears.

It's too far *for* your little legs.

These are **conjunctions**. There is an easy way to remember them with an acronym.

F	A	N	B	O	Y	S
For	And	Nor	But	Or	Yet	So

Conjunction	Meaning	Example
for	because	*I shall go to school <u>for</u> I need to study to become an accountant.*
and	also; in addition to	*I go to school in the morning <u>and</u> work in the afternoon.*
nor	connects two negative sentences	*He didn't speak <u>nor</u> did he smile.*
but	shows contrast	*My friend is naughty <u>but</u> her brother is well behaved.*
or	shows choice	*I will play <u>or</u> sit and study.*
yet	shows difference	*He was poor, <u>yet</u> he is honest.*
so	as a result of	*I work hard <u>so</u> my teacher loves me.*

Use suitable conjunctions and rewrite the pairs of sentences as a single sentence.

1. I don't want to play with you. I will sit with you.

2. She helps everyone. She was a kind girl.

3. I had a good book. I misplaced it.

4. Rahul worked hard. He did well.

5. My mother cooks well. I can't even make a dish.

6. We can go to the bazaar. We can visit our friends.

7. I went to play. I returned soon.

8. I climbed the tree. My brother fell down.

9. I go for games coaching every day. I go for singing classes on Fridays.

10. You can meet me at school. You meet me at the library.

Punctuation

Comma

Study the use of commas in these sentences.

1. Taffy, we are miles away from home and I have forgotten to bring any extra spears.
2. They had filled his hair quite solid with mud, they had rolled him up and down on pebbles, they had sat upon him and had thumped him till he could hardly breathe.

Commas have several uses in English. Let us look at some of them.

Commas are used:

- to separate words or a group of words in a list.

Example: Unni bought a bag of potatoes, a packet of sugar, a dozen apples and some grapes.

- while addressing somebody.

Example: Can I help you, ma'am?

- after exclamatory words like well, yes, no, why, hello, hey, etc.

Example: Hello, how are you? Well, thank goodness you are all right!

- to include extra information in a sentence. In these instances, the sentences will have the same meaning even if the words set apart by commas are left out.

Example: The champaka tree, on which many birds nested, was older than all the other trees around ('on which many birds nested' gives additional information about the champaka tree; if we remove these words, the sentence would still have the same meaning).

Punctuate and rewrite the passage.

a terrible storm overturned a ship all fell into the sea a monkey was saved by a dolphin the dolphin carried him ashore to an island reaching there the dolphin asked the monkey do you know this place the monkey replied yes I do the king of the island is my best friend do you know that I am actually a prince the dolphin said so you are a prince now you can be a king the monkey asked how can I be a king that is easy said the dolphin as you are the only creature on this island you will naturally be the king

Write now

The tribe wishes to compensate the Stranger-man for their bad behaviour. But the man is missing. They want to make a poster describing him, so that they can thank him for being helpful. Draw and describe Stanger-man.

Remember that like adjectives, descriptions too, have an order.

- **Height:** tall; tallish; short; shortish; medium height
- **Build:** frail; stocky; slim; thin; plump; fat; skinny; well-built
- **Age:** young; elderly; middle-aged; teenager; in 20s; 30s; 40s
- **Face:** round; oval; square; with scars; wrinkles; freckles; sun-tanned; pale
- **Eyes:** big round blue eyes; large; small; bright; narrow
- **Hair:** bald; straight; curly; spiky; wavy
- **Clothes:** casual; scruffy; shabby; smart; tidy; messy

Communication corner

A. Listen to the passage and answer the questions given below.

1. The basic needs of the earliest humans were ....

2. They lived ....

3. The people who lived in the Old Stone Age ate ....

4. This age was called the Old Stone Age because ....

5. The greatest discovery for the people of the New Stone Age was ....

6. People built houses near ....

7. They started making ....

B. Look at the following images. Pretend you live in the Stone Age. How would these things help you? Discuss with a friend or the whole class.

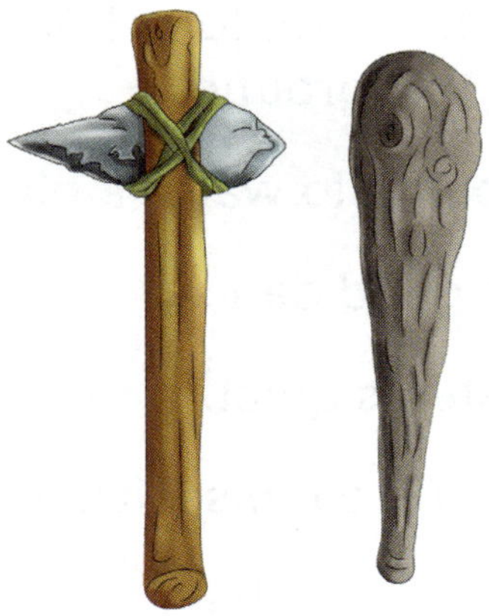

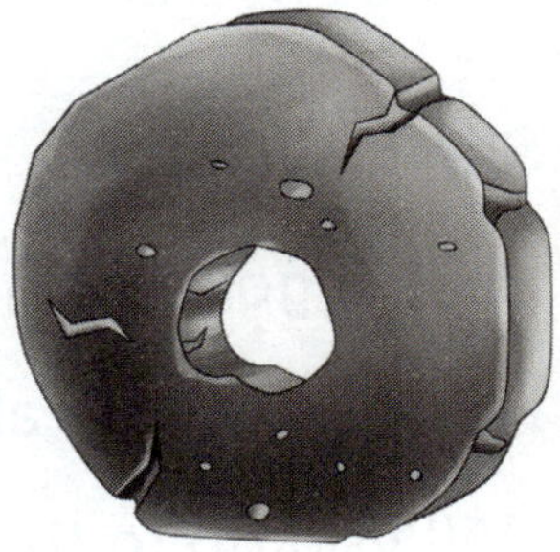

Worksheet 9

Grammar check

Conjunctions

There are seven coordinating conjunctions. These give equal importance to the words or sentences that these words connect.

and	but	or	nor	for	yet	so

Coordinating conjunctions are used for:

1. so – for showing the consequence of something
2. but – for difference
3. for – for explaining why
4. and – the same, similar or equal; without contrast
5. nor – for two non-contrasting grammatically negative items (not + not)
6. or – before an alternative
7. yet – contrast, despite something

A. Join the sentences using appropriate conjunctions. One has been done for you.

Sentence	Conjunction	Sentences
1. He was scared.	but	He practices for long hours on the playground.
2. She is talkative.	so	Will you go to watch a play?
3. He is a good singer.	for	He is a good dancer.
4. He doesn't eat cake.	or	Her sister is quiet.
5. Will you go to the market?	nor	He doesn't eat biscuits.
6. He is loved by all.	yet	He shouted for help.
7. He's unwell.	and	He is helpful.

1. He was scared so he shouted for help.

2. ....
3. ....
4. ....
5. ....
6. ....
7. ....

B. Complete the following sentences.

1. I went to the airport, and ....
2. Rita wanted to work, but ....
3. It was raining, so ....
4. I went to see my grandmother, so ....
5. Ali did not finish his work, nor ....
6. Mohan is very weak, yet ....
7. Will you go to Shimla or .... ?
8. I will come over tomorrow and ....
9. Did you like the film more or .... ?
10. Richa reached the party but ....

C. Fill in the blanks using the appropriate conjunction.

1. My sister .... I are going shopping today.
2. The man doesn't have much money .... he is always ready to help others.
3. Either the thief will be arrested .... he will manage to escape.
4. We are getting late .... you must hurry up.
5. He was a bully .... the students hated him.
6. I want to reach the station early .... we should leave soon.
7. It doesn't matter whether we win .... not.
8. We worked very hard .... we did not succeed.
9. Auritro was confused .... he volunteered to help.
10. I learnt how to speak Italian .... I could talk to my pen friend.

Write now

Study the poster given below.

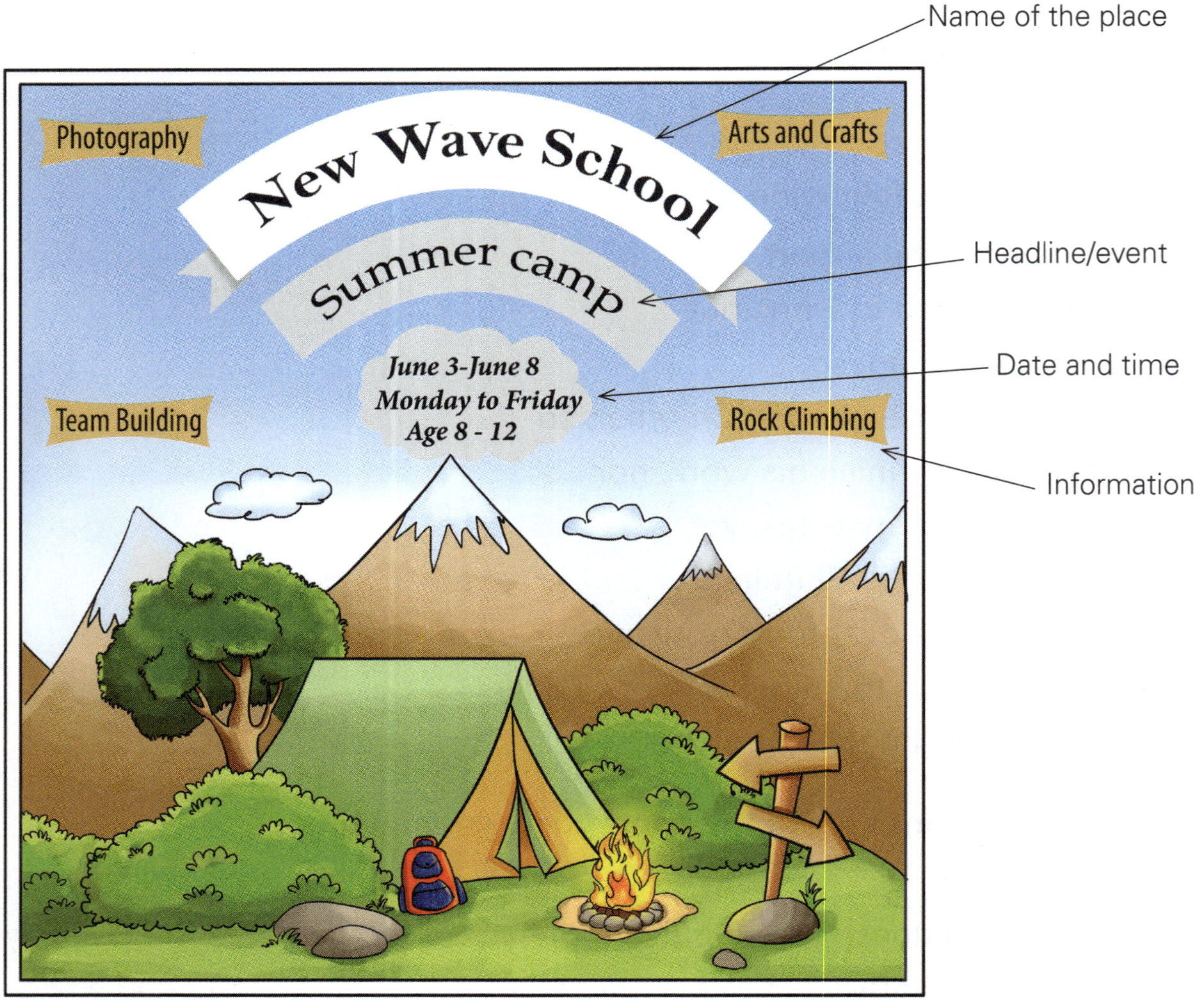

Then design and create a poster advertising a pet shop event. Remember to make it look appealing as well as informative.

REMEMBER:

- Information on what the event is (sale, petting day, fundraiser)
- Information on what can usually be bought there (what animals, their supplies)
- Description of the facilities available there (vets, grooming, day care)
- Venue/Contact information (name of the shop, address, number)
- Date and time
- An interesting caption/headline

Dear Mum

Have you ever twisted the truth just so you could get out of trouble? Here is a poem about a child who has done naughty things and has made up stories to tell his mother.

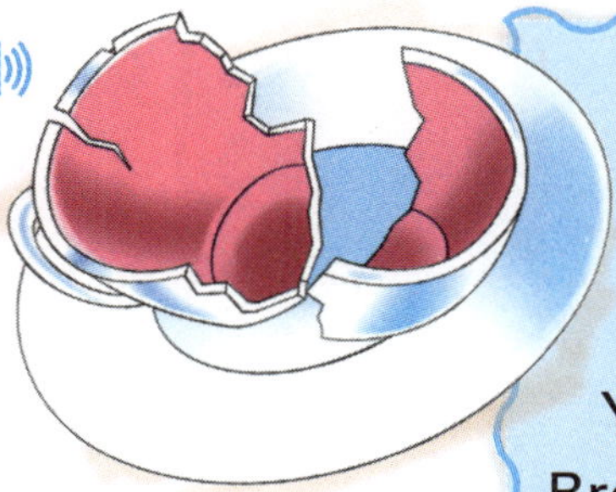

Dear Mum
While you were out,
A cup went and broke itself.
A crack appeared in that old blue vase
Your great-great granddad
Brought back from Mr Ming[1] in China.

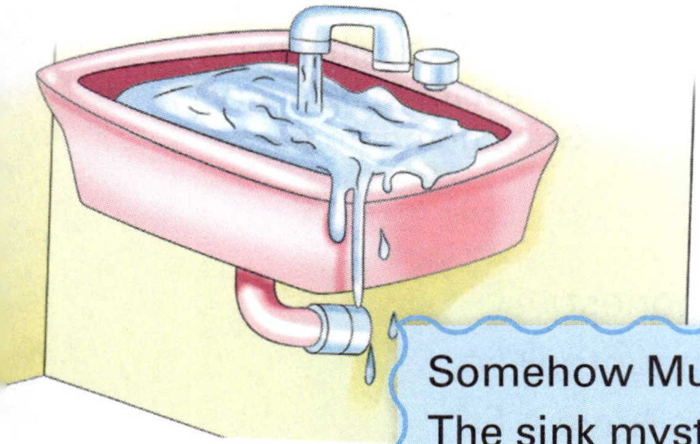

Somehow Mum, without me even turning on the tap.
The sink mysteriously[2] overflowed.
A strange jam stain about the size of a boy's hand,
appeared on the kitchen wall.

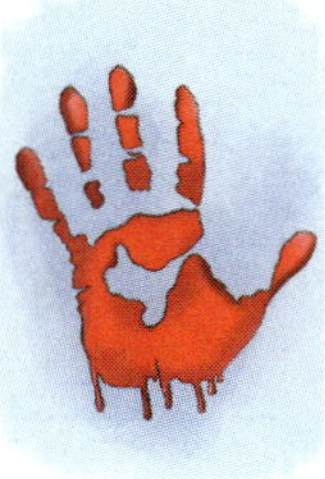

[1]**Mr Ming:** refers to the Ming dynasty which ruled China for 246 years | [2]**mysteriously**: in a way that is difficult to understand or explain

I don't think we'll ever discover
exactly how the cat
managed to turn on the washing machine
(especially from the inside)
Or how Sis's pet rabbit went and mistook
The waste-disposal unit for a burrow.

I can tell you, I was really scared when,
as if by magic,
a series of muddy footprints
appeared on your new white carpet.

[5]**haunted:** believed to be visited by ghosts | [6]**have a fit:** to be angry | [7]**Gran:** grandmother

I was being good (honest)
But I think the house is haunted[5] so,
knowing you are going to have a fit[6],
I've gone over to Gran'[7]s for a bit.

Brian Patten

Brian Patten, (1946—) is an English poet. He writes extensively for both children and adults. Patten's style is lyrical and has been described as a highly engaging performer. He has been known to give readings frequently.

Appreciation

1. Who has written this letter? To whom is it addressed?
2. The letter talks of a series of things that have gone wrong. List these.

The object	What happened to it
a. cup	
b. vase	
c. sink	
d. kitchen wall	
e. waste-disposal bin	
f. washing machine	
g. white carpet	

3. What does the speaker suggest is possibly wrong? Do you think he is telling the truth? VB
4. Where is the speaker now? Why is he there?
5. The poem is written quite unlike a poem. There are no rhyming patterns nor are the lines of equal length. Why do you think had the poet done this?
6. What do you think the speaker was doing while his mother was away?
7. Imagine you are the speaker of the poem. Write another letter to your mother confessing what actually happened. Before you start writing, think and plan what the possible reasons for each of these accidents could be. VB

   Example: He was running and knocked the cup down from the table.

You could begin like this:

Dear Mummy

I'm really sorry for misreporting the facts to you. I would like to confess

Activity

Make a list of ten different situations that would require excuses (in class or at home). Then create an excuse for each one of the situations. Afterwards, read out the excuses in class and discuss the most interesting excuse you have heard.